I GET LOUD

Copyright © 2021 by David Ouimet

For information about permission to reproduce selections from this book, write to
Permissions, W. W. Norton & Company, Inc., 500 Fifth Avenue, New York, NY 10110

For information about special discounts for bulk purchases, please contact
W. W. Norton Special Sales at specialsales@wwnorton.com or 800-233-4830

Manufacturing by Toppan Leefung Hong Kong
Book design by Angela Corbo Gier
Production manager: Anna Oler

Library of Congress Cataloging-in-Publication Data

Names: Ouimet, David, author, illustrator.
Title: I get loud / David Ouimet.
Description: First edition. | New York, NY : Norton Young Readers, an imprint of W. W. Norton & Company, 2021. |
Audience: Ages 6–8. | Summary: "Follows a girl learning to express herself and connect with others. How do you use
your voice, once you've finally found it? Growing in self-confidence, she befriends a stranger who becomes her
closest companion. Despite their differences, they speak and sing and laugh, their friendship weathering darkness
and light, stormy seas and calm waters"—Provided by publisher.
Identifiers: LCCN 2021005131 | ISBN 9781324004394 (hardcover) | ISBN 9781324004400 (epub) |
ISBN 9781324005308 (kindle edition)
Subjects: CYAC: Self-confidence—Fiction. | Friendship—Fiction.
Classification: LCC PZ7.1.O884 Iaf 2021 | DDC [E]—dc23
LC record available at https://lccn.loc.gov/2021005131

W. W. Norton & Company, Inc., 500 Fifth Avenue, New York, N.Y. 10110

www.wwnorton.com

W. W. Norton & Company Ltd., 15 Carlisle Street, London W1D 3BS

2 4 6 8 0 9 7 5 3 1

I GET LOUD

DAVID OUIMET

NORTON YOUNG READERS

An Imprint of W. W. Norton & Company
Independent Publishers Since 1923

Sometimes I get loud.

When I am swept into
the light of life,
I feel my heart lift.

So I get loud.

I see you,
will you see me?

You hear my song and
turn toward me.

You are small and brave;
with you, I feel free and loud.

I listen to you,
you to me.

We speak and sing.
We laugh and stutter.

Have you ever
screamed underwater

as loud as you could?

Don't you know that we
are louder
together?

Sometimes the wind
breaks what was bound.

We know how colors can fade

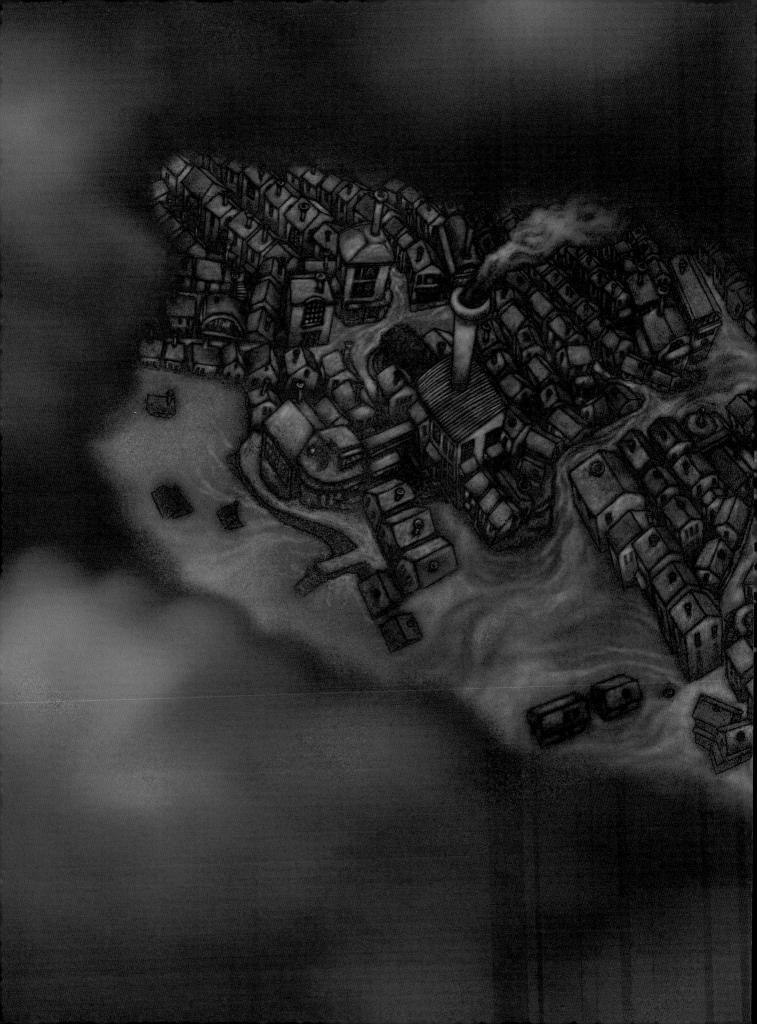

and light can drown

when our roots are pulled
from our broken ground.

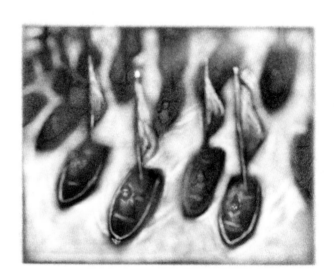

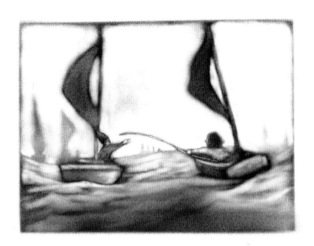

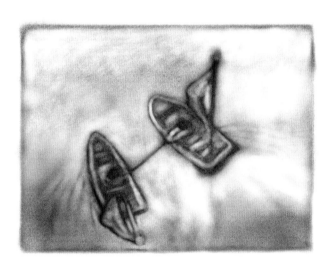

We were louder together.

Alone, I go quiet

Sometimes the wind
binds what was broken

In the jumble
of voices I hear

the only one I know.

I shout, you gasp.
I mew, you roar.

Our songs will rise,
our voices will surge,
because we are louder
together.

We are bound by endless stories.

Our sounds are stairs,
singing.

Our words are windows,
laughing.

Our hearts are our home, shimmering.
With you,
I get loud.